Sweating Tears
with Fat White Family

ROUGH TRADE BOOKS

Preface

You are about to read two candid interviews with Lias Saoudi and Saul Adamczewski, the singer and lead guitarist with Fat White Family. They were conducted in London and Leeds, in March 2019, a month before the release of their third album, *Serfs Up*. Formed in a Brixton squat eight years ago, the band has seen a revolving cast of 26 members and has mostly existed in continuous turmoil.

The band's early interviews often consisted of an argument and spilled into physical fights. At the time, there were few bands who dared behave like that in front of journalists, a fact that only made me like them more. Each album was chaotic and spiteful, with nerve-hitting lines and heavy, uncompromising arrangements.

In their promotional photographs they looked grubby, malnourished and *jolie laide*. Their video for *Auto-Neutron* featured raw steak, peepholes, bloody sinks and pigs' ears. It was squalid, hypnotic, and creepy. I was instantly captivated.

The songwriting partnership between Saul, Lias and his brother Nathan was fraught at the best of times. From this thin line of love and hate a batch of songs emerged that encapsulated not only the vitriolic personal dynamics of the band, but also the rising rage and seething political climate of contemporary British society under Conservative rule.

The vile affections that bind them are explored in this pamphlet. I considered it an opportunity to not only unknot some of their tangled personal history, but also to answer some of my own curiosity about the band. Perhaps it's the bitterness, humour and cruelty that I find so compelling, or the provocation, doomed lust and acerbic love songs.

As a youth I was obsessed by Channel 4's *Star Test*, where celebrities were questioned alone by a computer, choosing their intimate questions at will. *Sweating Tears* is my chance to live out that teenage fantasy on the page, except in this case I am the computer, using the seven deadly sins as a starting point. Thankfully, Lias and Saul didn't take much prompting, and were full of stories and wild tales from the road. I hope this gives you an introduction to one of Britain's most unpredictable live bands and provides a snapshot of their Orphean descent into the underworld.

Adelle Stripe, West Riding, 2019

Part One:

Lias Saoudi
Streatham, South London

It is 11.45am on a Sunday morning. I am walking along a dark corridor with Lias Saoudi, towards his bedroom. He has been at the sauna; his hair is damp and curly from the steam.

We push past drum kits, unopened mail and old mattresses; it's a place where no light exists. In one room the landlord is locked away with a glass pipe, chasing oblivion.

This is the house Lias calls home. We sit and laugh about the surroundings; his prison-regulation bed with perfectly made hospital corners, the dirty finger marks above the headboard, the stag beetle in a box frame, and the detritus of Lias' life gathering dust on the desk.

The window looks out onto an overgrown garden, where an inflatable swimming pool is filled with mud and leaves; convolvulus strangles each inch of soil. Next door, we can see an open suitcase of rotting potatoes, a rusty barbeque and plastic sunchairs. This is where lyrics are written.

I try not to stare too hard at the books, always an indication of a person's mettle— but Trocchi has pride of place, which comes as no surprise. We discuss the horror and beauty of Céline, Hamsun, Tolstoy, Zola, Genet and Huysmans. He is clearly a man with impeccable literary taste.

A laptop plays music from a small speaker; we listen to Arvo Pärt, Roy Orbison, eden ahbez, Lee Hazlewood and names I do not recognise. Our verbal derive is interrupted only by tea breaks, or an occasional love-bomb from Armani, the resident Staffordshire Terrier, who bursts through the door for a fuss. Her paws are soft, and I scratch behind her ears as she tries to climb onto my lap...

—My name is Lias Saoudi, born 22nd March 1986. We are sitting in my bedroom, in deepest darkest Streatham, in no man's land.

I'd describe myself as having a severely Roman nose, disproportionately grandiose. Today I'm wearing Mark Knopfler jeans, rancid squash court trainers, and a H&M Christmas jumper.

My hair's unkempt. I've been contemplating the monk cut again, it's hideous but I'm saving it up for the tour... I've noticed myself aging a little bit, although I'm sober most of the time now.

When I was an adolescent, like everyone else, I had horrendous self-image, but I feel alright about it now. I wish I had a little more sartorial *savvy*. Many of my friends are peacocks, but I've never been able to put the effort in.

Being narcissistic is inevitable. As a singer and making art, certainly being in a group, there's a quota of self-interest and self-observation that are the required critical faculties to do the job. You make this stuff and tear it to pieces. But I don't think I'm unreasonably vain.

I do feel relatively juvenile though. I'm living in a rented room, with few possessions; the idea of having a family, it's a million miles away to me. It's an unabashed, and shamefully bohemian existence. By the time my dad was this age he had three kids.

ⵣ

My mum's family are from Huddersfield. Working-class, salt of the earth, mining background. She met Dad in a nightclub. He was from Algeria, a town called M'Chedallah. He'd come over to study, she got knocked up, so that's how my older brother came into the world. But the whole thing was built on shaky foundations. Their marriage was a miserable, loveless affair.

Dad speaks to machines for a living, he educated himself. That will to propel myself further in the world, it comes from him.

Looking back, it was a brutal break-up. In my dad's culture divorce is not part of their vocabulary.

When he had his midlife crisis, just before his marriage fell apart, he got into Sai Baba (the guru) and flew to India to kiss his feet. This was the final straw for my mother. He still has a photograph of him above his bed. We thought it was fucking hilarious and ripped the piss out of him. Anything happened and we blamed it on Baba.

Growing up, my parents listened to music at home; Mum was into George Michael and Rod Stewart. But Dad liked Algerian folk, Aït Menguellet and Matoub Lounès, who was a Kabylie hero. They call him 'Le Rebelle', he was shot for his opinions. There's a museum dedicated to him with his car full of bullet holes. The sort of museum you'd only get in Algeria.

Out there he's a God. It's Zidane and Le Rebelle. One of his album covers had the crescent moon dripping with blood. He was pushing it. There's some of that in us, for sure. We had a hammer and sickle dripping with blood on our first album, *Champagne Holocaust*.

ⵣ

After my parents split up, we moved from Ayrshire out to Cookstown in Northern Ireland when I was twelve.

I was chronically shy, but slightly pompous, bullied, and ostracised from the local community. And arrogant in the sense that I thought everyone I was surrounded by was a troglodyte of the lowest order.

There was a deeply rooted sense of myself as being intellectually superior and cultivated in a way that they could never be. These were the hard facts. I constructed an escape plan very quickly.

I was so different; me and my brother were the racial minority. I had to learn how to fight. It was at the end of the Troubles, people spat in my face and called me a paki.

In the isolation of my youth I started to identify with music in an obsessive way. My girlfriend at the time lived on a Unionist estate, with murals painted on the houses in red, white and blue.

Her father was in the British army. He was the person who got me into music, but I learned a lot from her as well. She was the only person within five hundred miles who was into the same shit as me, a gift from God.

Once I met her, everything was fine. It didn't matter that I didn't have any friends, I didn't care anymore because I had her.

I was sad to leave, but I'd been offered a place at The Slade, studying fine art. Egon Schiele's writhing, tortured, hyper-sexualised images were an influence. I'd spend twenty hours drawing a tiny self-portrait in photographic detail and could render it perfectly. Because I was so isolated, and had no social life, I was studious and clued up on everything. Art was my way out.

When I arrived in London I felt like an outsider and missed the primitivism of Northern Ireland, the rough-hewn self-expression, without filters of etiquette.

When I think about it, all those rough knocks that happened to me as a young man, every time I get onstage, every fucking one of those things is in my head. Before I walk out at Brixton Academy, every dig, it's all in there.

⌘

I've played a few dreadful gigs over the years, but The Moonlandingz at Glastonbury was probably one of the most catastrophic hours I've ever spent on the stage.

I'd gone out to Shangri-La the night before after a poxy argument with Saul on the way down. He'd got himself on the bus, all smacky and pissy, in a shitty mood, being a bit of a prick, so I stormed off with my mate Scouse Chris wanting to forget about it.

I did an awful pill, was up all night being sick, and was onstage at 1pm the next day. I was shivering; all I wanted was a nice quiet room, instead I thought I'm never going to be able to do this, it's the worst pill comedown I've ever had…

One of my associates gave me a small bit of heroin—something I've dabbled with in the past (although I've never been a junkie)—I thought a bit of that will level me out. Even though every time I've ever done heroin, I spend an hour being sick immediately after I take it.

So, it's stage time in fifteen minutes and the matinee show at the Park Stage, full of families who have heard the record on 6Music. I get up on the stage painted entirely red, except for the word DAD on my forehead. I have a loaf of 50/50 Hovis clingfilmed to my head in a crown.

The first verse starts and I'm being sick on the stage; it happened about twelve times, between each verse. The band couldn't just cool it as it was all backing tracks, and I was singing through a growing pool of vomit. I kept catching glimpses of the audience, with their kids staring up at me, and I swear it was the longest hour of my life.

⌘

It's true that I once shat onstage, yes. That was in the early days of Fat White Family, when I had the fire in me. I was so angry with everything that night. We'd had ten years in the gutter, the abuse, being ignored, signing on, completely broke. By that point I just thought this is a laugh, people are buying tickets, we can do whatever we want.

Obviously, I'd looked at GG Allin, and thought I have to go there to know what *that* feels like.

It was our first full tour; I had no system so was just boshing pills and speed every night. On the fifth night, by the time we reached Sheffield, the reality of touring life was dawning on me...

I arrived there feeling fucked off. The venue only gave me one drink token saying I could have an ale or cider. I asked for a beer instead, but they said no. So, I was like fuck this, man, the venue was sold out, I thought right, we're going to have a dirty protest tonight. I'm going full Bobby Sands.

I was wearing a suit with a tie, got onstage, pulled my trousers down, cupped my hand, had a really runny tour shit into it, then I wiped it on my face. The band had no idea I was going to do it. I finally had Saul in his place.

The band were all kicking me away. The only person who didn't notice was Adam, who was on so much junk at the time that it didn't register. So, I started to tongue him, and he still didn't notice. I mean, it fucking stank. But it was like having a forcefield; I was Moses walking through the crowd that were parting.

One guy was so out of it he put me on his shoulders, so I took my belt off and was whipping him like a horse. It was next level, I'm proud of it.

☿

I guess I have a quasi-religious dedication to making art. That's been there since I was little. It's a no-brainer. Humans need religion and art. And money.

I was out in Algeria last year, fasting for Ramadan. I couldn't do it properly as I don't have Allah. If I had a proper object that I was obsessed with then I could focus, and it might just work. But as a westerner who's already a bit of a glutton I only lasted four days.

It's the antidote to London and this lifestyle. Their culture and the way they live is so peaceful, the opposite of here. When we started writing songs a lot of it happened in Algeria.

Our first band, The Saudis, we were always the bottom of the bill at New Cross Inn on a Tuesday night. We couldn't play, so we decided to go out to my gran's house for three months to write, in her garage.

It was in a small town, surrounded

by olive groves, at the foot of the Djurdjura, in the Tell Atlas mountain range in Kabylie. It's a beautiful place and good hash of course. We wrote *Touch the Leather* out there, it's a place to get in tune with your mind.

I came back here for three months after visiting and thought it was disgusting. The advertisements and sex; this place is like Babylon. It's so flawed and temporary, impulse-based and sensory.

It made sense to me then. Their way of life is built on reflection and meditation. But at that point I hadn't been back to Algeria for ten years. It made me think there's something to be said for this other way.

ⵣ

My Algerian family all go to the mosque. They are Berbers, from a culture that's distinctive in its own right; but was hijacked by Islam. It's been around for 6000 years and has its own language.

My grandad, Kaci, was vehemently anti-Islam, he'd been imprisoned in French Guyana for life for murdering a Frenchman when he was seventeen.

He was a smart and studious kid, and an accountant had hired him to be his assistant. His two cousins got wind and were jealous of the privileges he was enjoying, so they decided to rob and kill the accountant.

Apparently, Grandad didn't stick the knife in, but he took responsibility. Instead of the guillotine they sent him to Devil's Island. It's the same prison as the one in *Papillon*.

He was in there for 25 years, but his two cousins died inside after a couple of years. One in ten survive a life sentence in that place. When he was released, he came home and started a family. He was probably quite fucked up from all of that.

When my dad was little, he stole some money out of his desk with his brother, and Grandad put a shotgun up against both of their heads... this is why I have a problem with what the media describes as "emotional abuse." I'm like, come on man, I'll tell you all about emotional abuse.

ⵣ

I'm certainly not a sex person in a Brian Eno, five-times-a-day or collapsed lung sense. But it's the core thing in terms of what I write about. I look for sexual connotations in everything. It's to do with power. In terms of my actual sex life I'm disappointingly prudish.

My last serious relationship was ten years ago, I made a real mess of it. And then I started cheating on her, she cheated on me, and we had a year-long war of sexual attrition. It just got more and more brutal.

Since then I've just had these transactional soulless operations that expose a lack of guts and faith in the whole process.

Being in a touring band is like being in the Navy. You can't have a relationship; I have tried, but it's always a complete disaster. It's better if I'm alone.

To some extent I am ruled by lust. In my twenties I had to be out taking drugs and shagging, otherwise I wasn't living. It was the only way I could validate myself. It wasn't a good night unless it ended with *that*. It was a fixation. Aren't all young men that way inclined? Well, that's wrong because Nathan and Saul aren't like that. They were into heroin instead. A voracious appetite for women was mine.

The songs I'm really proud of, nine times out of ten were a reaction to something that was going on with my relationship with Saul. I realised afterwards that I was documenting it. In some ways you could say that he was a muse. But it's tied to that sense of conflict, power and competition.

⚥

Throwing yourself into a chaotic, un-expected situation is often the most inspiring thing you can do. Or even a shitty job. One of the most abysmal I ever had was at the meatpacking plant in Cookstown, where you had to start at 5am and work in a giant freezer, putting slabs of meat onto a tray.

I was on this conveyor belt, with hundreds of other guys, and you couldn't stop until the order was finished, time would just stretch out.

But the very worst had to be the National Maritime Museum in Greenwich. I was an invigilator, and I'd been signing on for so long that they made me do it, otherwise I'd lose my dole.

I breezed the interview because I thought I could just sit and read a book. But you weren't allowed to sit, and you weren't allowed to read either. And nobody goes there because it's a bit crap, full of boats and anchors.

There was one room dedicated to the history of time pieces, full of fucking clocks, old, new and digital. And I'd stand for eight hours, with a clip-on tie, nobody came in, but if you sat down on a chair, they'd see you on a camera and tell you to stand up.

At least in the factory I had a physical role, and it had a whiff of Springsteen about it, romantically awful, but this was like watching my life being counted down on all sides. The clock room on an MDMA comedown was torturous.

〄

When I lived out in Hollywood for a while, I have never seen so much misery as there is right there up at the top. Every story I have heard about that world is sinister. There are no more taboos. They own everything, take private jets everywhere. You know, what's left that isn't mine?

It was an education spending time behind closed doors out there. I didn't feel inferior, my natural-born superiority complex was there, and if anything inflamed by realising how thick most of these people are. Not only are they vile sadists but they are total morons who have never read anything.

You can't sit and have a conversation with these people, for the most part they are complete idiots. But from a purely anthropological view it was priceless.

We are talking about wealthy people who fly all over the world to Paris, New York, India and think they know everything. But they are hypocrites, living in houses like the Turbine Hall, with babbling brooks running through the living room, in the middle of a Californian drought.

They don't know what poverty and hardship is. On the day Trump got in part of me was glad. I was like, there you go! That's what you get. *Wake up!*

When Kanye went into the president's office and started banging on about building a Gucci spaceship, it was priceless. That's what I want out of a popstar. I don't care if he's left or right, if you go to popstars for your political orientation then you're a fucking tool.

〄

I shy away from conflict in everyday life, I struggle with it, but I'm violently competitive. It's part of my upbringing, the Algerian-Yorkshire background, three brothers and all that. Displacement when I was young. That's fed into this thing within me that has to crush the opposition. I don't see other groups as individuals with feelings, they are just contrary symbols that need to be dissolved.

In terms of our 'success', well, look how I'm living. But we are a successful band in the sense that our approach, attitude and sense of resentment has passed on to a new generation. For us it's a case of surviving our imitators.

I mean, what have we done? They

are all so young. The music industry has looked at us and thought, right, if we can just get a bunch of twenty-year-olds to be a bit like that, but not as difficult... You see, without the difficulty it doesn't amount to anything. You have to be willing to upset people. We live in a culture right now where that is not permissible. You can't say this; you can't say that. I mean, that's your job.

You need people like me out there, prepared to humiliate themselves in the public field so you can bounce conversations around. I'm a totem of humiliation and you should be grateful of that service for the whole community. I'm doing it so you don't have to. Give me some credit.

☉

If I had real money, I'd use it to wage a cultural war and further my vision of the world, and push it onto other people, because I'm right and they are wrong.

I'm permanently at war with everybody on one level, and I must have made some enemies, but even though I haven't made any money, and things are difficult, I feel happy, and that life has been fairly good to me. There's been conflict, but at the same time I feel grateful.

As for genuine adversaries, the closest thing is Saul. But he's also my best friend. That's a healthy rivalry that bears fruit. Depending on the conversation we've had at any given time I think that's the closest thing I have to an enemy.

Saul's got a reputation. Music industry people can't understand why I put up with it. It's essential to the aesthetic life of the band, that's why. Otherwise I'd become an egotist. It requires humility to absorb the most ferocious kind of criticism at all times.

I don't mind arguing with him as it's essential to have that incredibly cynical and bitter voice. That's where the real power lies.

For this record, Nathan's been writing songs, so there was a three-way which made it particularly bloody. It was like the Italian landings. Suddenly Saul was at war on two fronts.

☉

When it comes down to the actual collaborative part of creativity then I'm pretty good at removing my ego. Which is why when it's all done and I'm out in the public sphere I can be as seemingly egotistical as I feel like.

I can be very nurturing, but Saul's role in the band is the vexatious neglectful father, and I'm the battered housewife.

I nearly had a fight with him two weeks ago; he always throws the first punch. But he's no good at fighting, that's for sure. Larry Love from Alabama 3 once saw us have a proper fight in the Queen's Head in the middle of the day, Saul kept demanding that I carry his guitar for him, and I just flipped.

It's like watching two stick insects go at each other. Pathetic. It's a good job neither of us can do much damage. He's tried to gouge my eye out, smash my head in with a bottle; we've had loads of altercations, but I'm not sure you'd class them as actual fights.

⌘

If I'm stressed and burned out, I can fall into a chasm of semi-suicidal feelings. It's rare but I can have days where I just stare at the wall. You can't even feed yourself or put music on. At those times I have nothing but disdain for all human life.

It doesn't appear arbitrarily, there's usually a reason for it. My personality becomes quite toxic at that point, so I just isolate myself. Enforced quarantine until it's passed.

Horrible things have happened to me, my family, the band being hideous,

abusive relationships, but the bad stuff, it's all relative. I've never witnessed hell, or anything like it.

After what happened to Dale Barclay last year, that's the first experience I've had of death in my life. Somebody who I care about, who's close to me, dying from a terminal disease. And that experience of seeing him like that, spending time with him and his wife, was the ultimate moment of putting things in perspective.

I thought being in the Fat Whites was like some sort of Vietnam, so fucking dark, but seeing that made me realise it's all just a game. Watching what Dale went through, the struggle of it, I still think about him every day. That was real pain.

Part Two:

Saul Adamczewski
Leeds, West Yorkshire

The back room of the Brudenell Social Club is quiet today. To my left, a crusty couple drink slow pints, and roll cigarettes from a tobacco pouch. Outside, a car drives past playing heavyweight dub that almost reaches through my feet. It feels unnerving to be back here, after leaving Hyde Park twenty years ago, swearing never to return.

Saul Adamczewski walks into the empty venue with Alex White, saxophonist with Fat White Family, who is playing flute at his acoustic solo gig tonight.

Later on, I will listen to them perform delicate songs that Joe Boyd would be proud of, including a ballad based on Wakefield's most infamous dickhead, Paul Sykes, and another beauty, Gazza's Tears. The folk crowd will visibly wince at the lyrics, whilst others whisper-laugh into their pints, making secret smiles at each other. But all of that is for later.

Right now, I am watching Saul drag an amplifier across the stage. I give him a comic book by a non-woke American pervert, and we hitch a ride into the city.

He isn't looking too dishevelled today, all things considered. He was up until the early hours in a k-hole with a former Mancunian dominatrix who likes to mother him each time he visits.

His eyes are bigger than plates, wide as the day. It's the first thing you notice about him. Then, the clothes. He's one of those people who always looks stylish, regardless of the rags he is wearing. There is something familiar about Saul.

We travel to the centre of Leeds and emerge at the granite façade of the Henry Moore Institute, where Renee So's clay sculptures of inebriated characters line the gallery. Beneath the building is a vault, which we unlock and walk into...

—My name is Saul Adamczewski, I was born on the 28th of September 1988. I'd describe myself as kind of ghoulish looking. Sunken. Weathered.

I look in the mirror far too much. Yeah, I'm vain. Especially if you do a lot of junk. You can end up staring in the mirror for days, admiring what you see.

At one point I was in San Francisco waiting to go into rehab, in a hotel room for two weeks by myself with a Fentanyl prescription. I had a big pot of it and would eat three doughnuts and stare at myself, then keep changing my outfits.

The treatment was called Ibogaine, it was dreadful in some ways, but it was an insight. I was at one of the centres for a couple of months; they made me do gong baths and gave me toad poison. It was in Mexico initially, and that first week you are tripping for four days in a hospital bed.

It's exhausting to the point where after it had happened, I didn't really know who I was any more. That lasted for a couple of weeks. After it's finished, they just chuck you over the border and leave you to fend for yourself.

Five guys were there with me trying to get clean off heroin, we were let go at Tijuana, and one of them was going to give me a lift to LA.

I had no money, not even a phone, didn't even know my name. So, I got in this guy's van, and then all the others who had been at the centre got in as well, and the first thing they said was 'we're going to score.'

We were all still hallucinating. But the rest of them hated me and called me Inspector Gadget. I stupidly thought they would be artists. But they were military men. Fred Durst hats and muscles.

After they scored, they wouldn't give me any of their drugs. We were driving through the Californian desert and they were shooting up into their armpits in this tiny van. I remember physically trying to disappear.

I stayed clean for four or five months after that. For me it was a long time. One of the lengthiest stints I've had.

Sometimes I go to Norway and take Kratom. I get looked after out there and can't score heroin as it's in the middle of nowhere.

I've done some cold turkeys where I don't feel any better for it at all. Then others where you get over the hump of the physical withdrawal suddenly you can start thinking again. You have clarity and remember who you are. And because I'm out there alone I can wander through the forests and meditate. I always have a deluge of ideas and songs.

✶

I first took heroin when I was working on a building site, with a guy who used to be my babysitter. I always looked up to him and thought he was cool.

We lived on Lyndhurst Grove in Peckham, and he used to go to the shop and buy us chocolate bars. He was sort of a family friend; the first time I saw anyone doing drugs it was him taking speed when I was about thirteen.

Later, I ended up working on this building site with him as a roofer. He'd invite me back to get on it. One day he said, 'you know we're going to do real drugs tonight, have you ever done it before?' and I just lied and said 'yeah, yeah...'

Then I'd go there every night after work, but I didn't have any idea how to even smoke heroin, he'd do it all for me. Eventually I realised he was getting me

to buy it, giving me nothing on the foil, and keeping it all to himself. I thought it was mild; that's because I wasn't getting any. But that's how the routine started, heroin and crack, then going back to work the next day.

One day I threw up from the roof all down the side of the house we were working on. It made shifts more tolerable, most certainly.

✶

My parents met when they were teenagers, living on Camberwell Grove. Mum was mates with Dad's little sister. Apparently, she was lying on the floor and he just walked in naked, got something out of her room and left. They weren't together very long and got divorced after I was born.

She was a single mum, but never had any permanent relationships after that. I grew up with her in Tulse Hill, on Romola Road. Then I'd go to my dad's every time I got kicked out.

From all accounts, as a five-year-old I was quite disturbed; violent and moody. I've always been the same. There's not much change with who I am now. They called me 'Naughty Saulie'.

I ran away a lot as a child; I'd sleep rough for a couple of nights then go home the next morning. Sometimes I'd go off on my bike to Brockwell Park, wearing a big jacket, steal Mum's fags, and smoke them through the night in a bush by myself. I'd take the big clock off my bedroom wall and put it in a bag, so I knew what time it was. I had fantasies of being Tom Sawyer.

As a kid I used to smash the classroom up. I have a volatile personality and can be violent. I reach a point where I have no control. And I've always been like it. It's a short fuse. But it's also to do with the way I was brought up.

I was surrounded by that behaviour; it feels normal to me. And once you've pushed that far and made peace with yourself, it's hard to go back. You accept that there's a part of you that can do that, and you try to be ok with yourself despite of it.

⚹

I like my own company more and more as I get older. When I was younger, I couldn't bear it. I was never one of those people who could go travelling by themselves.

When I was nineteen, I moved to Vienna. Lias and Nathan kicked me out of The Saudis, and I had a great-uncle that lived there. But I'd been to a free school in Vienna for a bit. It was like a Summerhill, with no rules.

I thought it was great, but I didn't learn anything or do any work. It was good in the way that if kids were really interested in gardening, for example, then they made a whole curriculum based on botany for them to study.

All these kids who were passionate about things, they would flourish. Then there was a bunch of us who were wasters, into smoking weed and skateboarding. Everyone had a vote, we even voted out our maths teacher.

I was eventually voted out of the school by the pupils. I'd made friends with the kids in the year above me. We were cool, and we were mean to the other kids. We were bullies, yes. But more like teasing, winding people up. I deserved to be kicked out.

Around that time when you saw me at Warwick Gardens as a teenager, I was regularly beaten up. Especially being little punks; we'd sit in the park by the station, me and my mate Freddie would play Discharge out of a boombox, drinking cider, then we'd get attacked by rude boys.

For years we were scared to be out on the streets. I was always so nervous about getting beaten up that I could see it coming before anyone else and scarpered. My friends were hospitalised, we had knives pulled on us, but I was always the one that got away.

✳

I used to get arrested for possession all the time in my twenties. There was a policeman who knew me, and I'd walk from the Hermit's Cave (where I used to drink), and I'd always have coke on me. He busted me three times. It got to the point where it was harassment.

The last time was in Heathrow Airport. I was supposed to go in for an interview as I'd threatened to kill someone on the internet, in a message. I didn't mean it *literally*, then they said they were going to call the police. I apologised but they'd already called it in.

So, I was supposed to talk to the police about this death threat, which wasn't a death threat, and I didn't go. And I kept going to Paris and didn't get arrested, but I walked into Heathrow on my way to New York and they had a mugshot of me when I was last nicked at twenty-one.

I was supposed to be recording with Insecure Men in New York, and Ben (Romans Hopcraft) had to fly without me. I had all this Oxycontin and Valium in my pockets, so in the cell, when their backs were turned, I necked all the pills. They didn't see me. I felt good after that. Nothing came of it, they didn't have any staff to interview me, so they let me go and booked me on the next flight. I got on the plane really high.

My first band was The Metros, and the only country where we had any following was Japan. The day before we were supposed to fly, I disappeared. I was on the way to the airport, and I got off the train at Crystal Palace, went and sat in the park, and turned my phone off.

I was too scared to get on a plane, but I didn't want to tell them. They were all waiting at the airport for me.

Eventually my manager found me, took me to a hypnotist, gave me sedatives, and put me on a flight the next day. After that I didn't fly again for six years. But with the Fat Whites I had to start flying again. Nathan's scared as well, we just sit there together and cling to the seat. Diazepam helps, but you can get hooked on it easily. Withdrawing from that can be harder than coming off heroin.

✳

I don't always enjoy playing live. Maybe one in every fifteen gigs. When we first started, at every gig we'd lose our shit, jumping over the bar, there was a period where each show we did was the most fun thing I've ever done in my life.

It was spontaneous, but genuine as well. I had no hang-ups about behaving like that. It's inevitable that if you are playing the same songs you get bored of it.

There was a period when I kept walking offstage after one or two songs. I'd had enough, was angry with everyone.

At one gig I fucked my guitar towards the end of the set, then hit Nathan's keyboard, broke it, and stormed off. I thought they'd all come with me, but half of them stayed on.

Then Lias started to play guitar and sang *Bomb Disneyland*, and I started bottling him from the side of the stage. It was in Nottingham; Jason from Sleaford Mods was there. I had to get them off.

I have sabotaged gigs as well, one time I pulled the mains while they were still playing. This kid got up and started playing my guitar and he was terrible, so it had to be done...

✳

I'm a dreadful insomniac. I get into a cycle where I can only fall asleep at midday, then the patterns start getting later. I'll stay up until six, then seven, and eventually it's a full circle, but somehow it re-jigs itself.

I had nightmares as a kid. With smack you have these dreams that are insane. They are always sexual but I'm not really a sexually motivated person. To be honest I'm more of a crack in the door / Peeping Tom in my natural state. I'm so shit at meeting new people and get tongue-tied. I'm not a smooth operator.

A lot of young men that I spend time with, every single night they are on this mission. And I was never interested in anything like that. I've always had girlfriends, relationships.

When I was first in love, that was a blissful time. She was called Lotte; I was about thirteen. There was some family rivalry there and her mother hated me.

We lost our virginity together, then her mother found out and we weren't allowed to see each other anymore. It was ten snatched minutes here and there; a secret romance.

As far as relationships go, I'm not jealous. I'm envious of other people though. But not sexually or in the sense of wanting to have ownership of others. I don't have enemies, but plenty of people I dislike. At a certain age it's good to have them.

Selfishness and laziness are my

worst attributes. I also have something in me from my mum's side which is this willingness to withdraw from social life. Cowardice is another.

I'm a sadist; definitely. Lias says he's a masochist, but I don't know. He's got a heroic complex going on. A real martyr.

✳

When it comes to food, I'm a glutton. I really love cooking and can do it well. My dad's a chef and had a restaurant. Everyone in the family is into food.

My death row meal would have to be a steak and kidney pudding, made with suet. I'm a big fan of offal, although I'm not against veganism, but I can't live like that.

I tried to cook a pie on Christmas day, a recipe from St. John. I go whenever I can afford it. The chef there is a fan, he looks after me. But the pie I attempted was a disaster.

I was cooking for French people who are snooty about English food, and I fucked it up. I wanted to impress them, but our fridge broke. I'd made a pastry, and jelly out of trotters, but it wouldn't come together.

I got so angry, like a kid at his own birthday party, and started shouting. I was embarrassed after that and couldn't even enjoy it.

My family are all big drinkers, but you can lose your taste for it on junk. I haven't been a proper drinker for a few years.

Since the Queen's Head shut down my appetite for it has gone. It was a pub in Brixton where we all used to live and hang out. Me, Lias and Nathan were photographed on the roof there at Thatcher's Death Party, with a banner that said: 'The Witch is Dead'.

The next day it was on the front page of the newspapers. It was a proud morning when we saw that. We were like 'we've finally done it, boys!'

✳

I've started getting into collecting tin soldiers recently. For the King Kong film in the 1930s, they made these soldiers, so I have some of them. And Mussolini, all the Italian fascists.

I also collect British celebrity paedophile memorabilia. I bought this Gary Glitter picture disc, on its own stand. It was £2. They're the dark lords of the 1970s, taking it all a bit too far. My girlfriend goes nuts about it, it freaks her out, so I have to hide it in the cupboards.

I would love to be big enough to play at the Royal Festival Hall with an orchestra. Or buy a flat. In some ways

I do lust for getting to that point. But not in a way that I want to be famous. I'd feel uncomfortable with it.

When I go to The Windmill in Brixton, to see some band play, that's the nearest I get to it. People recognise you and everyone comes up to talk.

On a good night maybe that's alright. Lias loves it, he's very *very* good at it. Sometimes it can be uncomfortable, so I'd hate to be famous.

Being a musician is always what I wanted to do. Aged fifteen I was into Pete Doherty and wanted to be in a band, I thought he was the coolest. So, in a tragic way I have fulfilled my dreams.